Nobody

Liz Rosenberg

Illustrated by Julie Downing

A NEAL PORTER BOOK
ROARING BROOK PRESS
NEW YORK

For Eli, who had Nobody for a long time.
For Lily, who came along at last and is Somebody.
And for David, who is Everything.
–L. R.

To Marie Robinson, librarian extraordinaire.
–J. D.

Text copyright © 2010 by Liz Rosenberg

Illustrations copyright © 2010 by Julie Downing

A Neal Porter Book

Published by Roaring Brook Press

Roaring Brook Press is a division of Holtzbrinck Publishing Holdings Limited Partnership

175 Fifth Avenue, New York, New York 10010

www.roaringbrookpress.com

Distributed in Canada by H. B. Fenn and Company Ltd.

Library of Congress Cataloging-in-Publication Data is on file at the Library of Congress

ISBN: 978-1-59643-120-1

Roaring Brook Press books are available for special promotions and premiums.
For details contact: Director of Special Markets, Holtzbrinck Publishers.

First Edition June 2010

Book design by Jennifer Browne

Printed in September 2009 in China by SNP Leefung Printers Ltd., Dongguan City, Guangdong Province

1 3 5 7 9 8 6 4 2

When George awoke early one Sunday morning, Nobody was up and about.

George's mom and dad were still asleep. Flo lay snoozing on the rug.

It was still dark outside. Even his mother's finches were sleeping in their cage.

Light was just beginning to streak across the sky.

Nobody said, "Up! Up! Up!"

Nobody said, "It's a beautiful day."

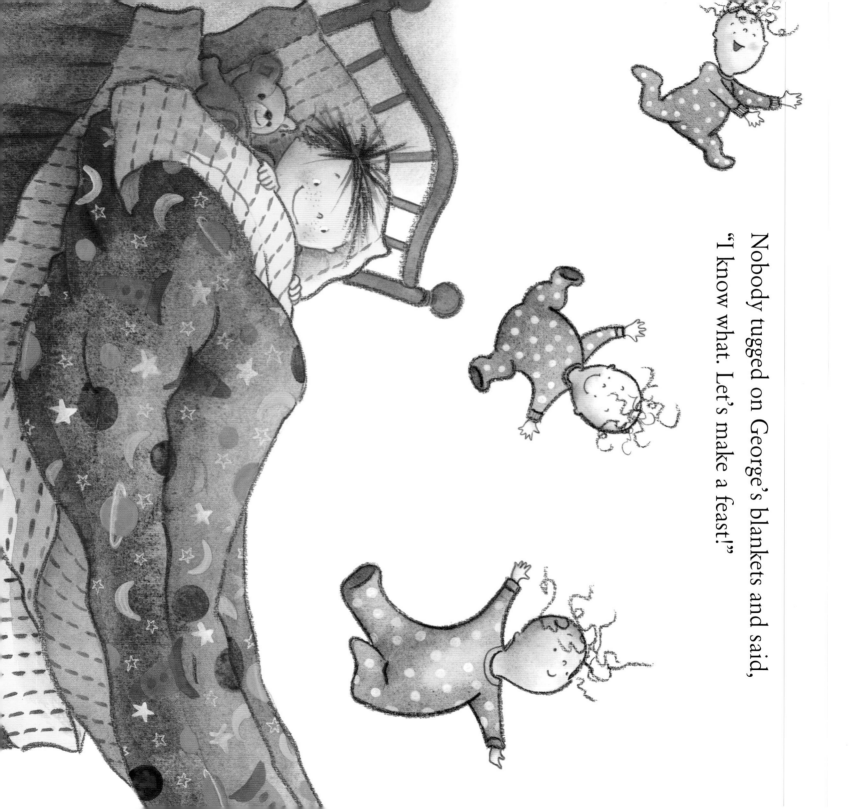

Nobody tugged on George's blankets and said,
"I know what. Let's make a feast!"

George was a very good cook. He sometimes made four-layer banana fudge sandwiches and Nobody cheered him on.

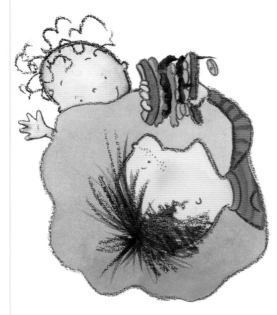

With Nobody's help he created amazing ice cream sundaes topped with cocoa, cherries, and mountains of whipped cream.

"Let's see," George said, peering into the refrigerator. "What looks good?"

Nobody made ridiculous suggestions. Chocolate meatloaf! Peanut butter and turnip soup! Spaghetti and applesauce dumplings!

George took out a dozen eggs, cracked them into a bowl, and mixed them up with a fancy eggbeater. Some of the eggshells got into the bowl. Nobody took them out.

George had helped his father make omelets, so he knew you needed lots of ingredients.

Nobody helped him take everything out of the fridge.

Nobody sorted things into piles.

George selected some of his favorite foods. He took out some things his mom and dad liked and some that Nobody wanted.

Flo hurried downstairs to see what was going on.

So George decided to add a few of her favorite treats.

Nobody called
out words of
encouragement.

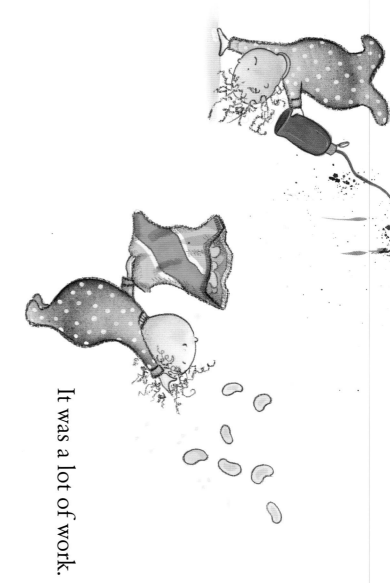

It was a lot of work.

Nobody mopped up the first few mistakes.

Then George sat and waited because he wasn't allowed to turn on the stove when Nobody was around.

While he waited, George played Go Fish and Nobody won.

George invented a new game called Jamaican Chee-Bop

and won.

Nobody got mad.

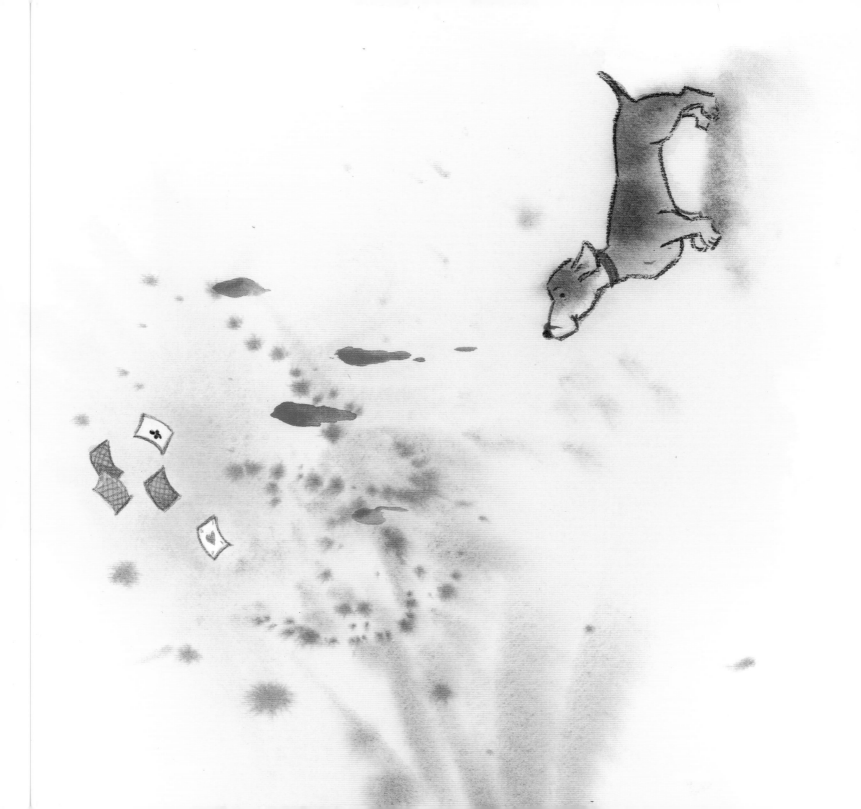

"Good heavens,"
said George's father.

"Good gracious,"
said George's mother.

"Almonds, anchovies, apricots," she mumbled.

"Pineapple, sweet potato, puppy treats . . .

George, what were you thinking?"

Then she saw the look on George's face and gave him a squeeze. "Wow. You did all this by yourself? It smells amazing down here! But," she added, kissing the top of his head, "I was really in the mood for pancakes. Do you think you could help me make some?"

"But of course," answered George. "Pancakes are my specialty."

"Then let's get started," she said.

That's when Nobody got smaller.

And smaller. Small enough
to get lost in George's pocket.

George thought how it had been Nobody's idea to make breakfast in the first place. He remembered how Nobody had been there to greet him that morning.

He thought about how alone he might have felt if there had been no one instead of Nobody around.

"Mom," George said. "Nobody helped me with this."

"Is that so?" said his mother, passing him a clean mixing bowl. George's father began washing up.

"Yes," said George. "And Nobody makes better pancakes than I do."

Nobody smiled a surprised sort of smile and started to grow a little bit.

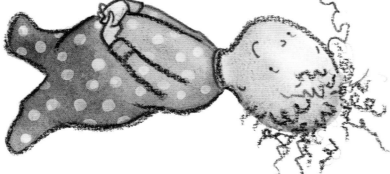

"Absolutely Nobody."

Then they all settled down to a delicious feast.

And Nobody ate more than George.